D0604481

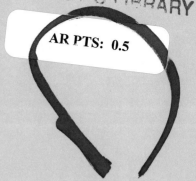

AR PTS: 0.5

Snow Day

by **Lynn Plourde**

illustrated by **Hideko Takahashi**

SIMON & SCHUSTER BOOKS FOR YOUNG READERS
New York • London • Toronto • Sydney • Singapore

SIMON & SCHUSTER
BOOKS FOR YOUNG READERS

An imprint of Simon & Schuster Children's Publishing Division
1230 Avenue of the Americas, New York, New York 10020

Text copyright © 2001 by Lynn Plourde
Illustrations copyright © 2001 by Hideko Takahashi
All rights reserved including the right of reproduction in whole or in part in any form.
SIMON & SCHUSTER BOOKS FOR YOUNG READERS is a trademark of Simon & Schuster.

A special thanks to Maine's poet laureate, Baron Wormser—L. P.

Book design by Paula Winicur
The text of this book is set in Graham.
The illustrations are rendered in acrylic on illustration board.
Printed in Hong Kong
2 4 6 8 10 9 7 5 3 1
Library of Congress Cataloging-in-Publication Data
Plourde, Lynn.
Snow day / by Lynn Plourde ; illustrated by Hideko Takahashi.—1st ed.
p. cm.
Summary: Children enjoy all kinds of activities inside and out on a snowy day.
ISBN 0-689-82600-1
[1. Snow—Fiction.] I. Takahashi, Hideko, ill. II. Title.
PZ7.P724 Sn 2001
[E]—dc21
00-063574

With love to Mom—thanks for making the
magic of snow days last all year long
—L. P.

To Yuehchuan, whose first snow was a snow day
—H. T.

Yawn.
Hug the pillow.
A cozy, curled lump in the quilt.
Mama whispers, "Snow day, child."
The quilt bursts open.

Is it . . .

Could it . . .

Would it be?

Jump to window.
White. Blinding, shining white.
Covering trees. Blanketing bushes. Burying road.
White, glorious white . . . EVERYWHERE!

Twirl and giggle.
Dance-a-prance.
Snow day chant.
"There's no-o-o-o-o-o-o-o-o day like a sno-o-o-o-o-o-o-o-o-w day!"

Snow day breakfast.
Steamy oatmeal in a brown sugar 'n' cream bath.
Plumpy pumpkin muffins
Change butter chunks to butter ch-m-m-melts.
Snow day, yummy snow day.

Couch cuddle.
Share books. Share dreams.
Just for a moment a princess.
Just for a second a pilot.
Just for a breath a dragon.
Tee hee. Sniggle. Wiggly giggle.
Snow day, silly snow day.

Wooooo-ooooo!
Wild, whirling wind
Crashes limbs to lines.
Lights dance. Flick-a-lick.
Lights die. Flick-a-floooo.
Snow day, fierce snow day.

Fireplace huddle.
Checkers and chuckles.
Old Maid. Go Fish.
Card castle. Pooooooof!
Snow day, playful snow day.

Cupboard carousing.
Hot chocolate. Mushy marshmallow dunk.
Popcorn, peanuts, pretzels.
Chocolate chips minus the cookies.
Yum! Smunch! Crunch!
Snow day, munchy snow day.

Papa's long johns.
Rainbow scarf. Nubby mittens.
Pom-pommed, pulled-down cap.
Snow day, bundly snow day.

Snowballs. Whoosh! Whoosh!
Snowman. Pat-a-slap.
Sled. Kwoosh! Thud! Trudge!
Snow angel. Plop! Snow fort. Hmmmpf!
Snow day, noisy snow day.

Snow day walk.
Sluggingly, trudgingly slow.
Snow day shovel.
Grunt, push, pick up, pwoosh.
Snow day tunnel.
Dig, digger, diggest.
Snow day dare.
Tippy, tippier, tippiest.
Snow day, busy snow day.

Deepening darkness.
Shake and shudder.
Stomp, clomp indoors.
Dripping, drenching. Hang to dry.
Snow day, shivery snow day.

Soapy soak.
Boat-filled bath.
Towel wrap.
Flannels with footies.
Snow day, snuggly snow day.

Steaming, stirring, bubbly broth.
Pinch-a-this. Pat-a-that.
Kit and caboodle stew.
Fluffy, flaky biscuits, too.
Snow day, warming snow day.

Rocking chair snuggle. Papa cuddles.
Mama whispers, "Snow day, child."
The quilt closes and quiets.
Child nestles with Mama.
Snow day melts to dreams.
Snow day, sleepy snow day.